HARLEQUIN BUTTERFLY

TOH ENJOE is a Japanese author of literary, scientific, and speculative fiction. Born in Hokkaido, he studied physics and mathematics and worked as a researcher and at a software firm before becoming a full-time writer. He has received several awards for his fiction, including the Noma Prize for New Writers, the Nihon SF Taisho Award, and the prestigious Akutagawa Prize for *Harlequin Butterfly*.

DAVID BOYD is assistant professor of Japanese at the University of North Carolina at Charlotte. He has translated novels and stories by Hiroko Oyamada, Masatsugu Ono, and Mieko Kawakami, among others. His translation of Hideo Furukawa's *Slow Boat* (Pushkin Press, 2017) won the 2017/2018 Japan-US Friendship Commission (JUSFC) Prize for the translation of Japanese literature.

TOH ENJOE

HARLEQUIN BUTTERFLY

Translated from the Japanese by
DAVID BOYD

PUSHKIN PRESS

Pushkin Press
Somerset House, Strand
London WC2R 1LA

Doukeshi no chou © 2015 EnJoe Toh. All rights reserved.
First published in Japan in 2015 by Kodansha Ltd., Tokyo.
Publication rights for this English edition arranged
through Kodansha Ltd., Tokyo

English translation © 2024 David Boyd

First published by Pushkin Press in 2024

Series Editors: David Karashima and Michael Emmerich
Translation Editor: Elmer Luke

Pushkin Press would like to thank the Yanai Initiative for Globalizing
Japanese Humanities at UCLA and Waseda University for its support.

◼ YANAI INITIATIVE

1 3 5 7 9 8 6 4 2

ISBN 13: 978-1-78227-977-8

Designed and typeset by Tetragon, London

Printed and bound in the United Kingdom by Clays Ltd, Elcograf S.p.A.

www.pushkinpress.com

HARLEQUIN
BUTTERFLY

First and foremost, for those whose names begin with A,
  with alpha, with aleph.
Then for those whose names begin with vowels,
  then B, and C, and down the list.
Through every order and classification,
  as defined by various rules and patterns
Where the net lands I cannot say, but could there be
  any other way?

I

WHAT ABOUT A BOOK THAT CAN BE READ ONLY WHEN travelling?

There's nothing exciting about a book that you can *also* read when travelling. There's a right time and place for everything, and anything that claims to work everywhere can only be subpar, some kind of sham.

A book that can be read only when travelling. It could be something like *The Book You Finish in Two Minutes while Doing a Headstand.*

The full force of the book would be lost on you unless you read it while upside down. You'd be able to follow the words on the page just fine while on your feet, but what you'd get out of it wouldn't be the same.

The text takes advantage of the rush of blood to your head.

As a variation on the same idea, you could create something like *Revelations Best Understood in a Fit of Anger.*

This happens in the air, between Tokyo and Seattle.

In my lap, I have the book I just bought at the airport: *Untold Tales for Those with Three Arms*. I try to read it, but nothing sticks. It's a recurring problem of mine. I don't know if it's the speed of the plane, but it feels like the words are struggling to hold onto the page, lagging behind and racing to catch up.

All I see on the page is a blur of ink. What's written there escapes me.

I give up and my mind wanders. I find myself thinking about books that could make use of the way the words move. I can never read when I'm travelling. I'll pack a couple of books, or maybe even buy a new one during the journey, but I can't think of a single time that I actually got anywhere with one of them.

I guess the ability to collect stray thoughts like these and turn them into money rather than words is what it takes to succeed in business.

A. A. Abrams might not have made billions, but he managed to amass a substantial fortune—and it all began with the businessman seriously entertaining one such flight of fancy.

This happens in the air, between Tokyo and Seattle.

Abrams is a man who more or less lives on passenger planes—not that he ever has a destination in mind. His business is conducted in flight. When circumstances keep him on the ground, he holes up in a hotel near the airport, ready to return to the air as soon as conditions permit. He's no flight attendant. Not a pilot, either. Just a passenger with nowhere to go.

He stuffs his corpulent frame into an economy-class seat, then waits for the layers of fat to settle into place. Once the plane has reached cruising altitude, fuselage and flesh in proper alignment, Abrams calls an attendant and orders two bottles of wine—one white, one red. Then he slowly removes a small item from the inner pocket of his coat: a bag made of silver thread wound around a glistening stick about the size of a ballpoint pen.

He frees the bag from the stick with his jumbo-sausage fingers. Then, with a motion that seems almost indecent, he opens the mouth of the bag—gently, like he's stroking the hair of a doll.

As if by magic, a tiny butterfly net appears between his hairy digits. Carefully bringing his index and middle fingers to his thumb, the Brobdingnagian giant pinches the net, making sure to hold it level.

He gives it a graceful wave, as if he were conducting his own humming.

Out of the corner of his eye, Abrams sizes me up in the seat beside him and squints at the book in my lap.

Certain that my attention is now his for the taking, he launches into a nonsensical spiel in a thick American accent:

"See this? I use this net to go around capturing fresh ideas. That's my trade. I've tried it out in all kinds of places, but nowhere beats a jumbo jet. When you're flying, all kinds of ideas pop into your head, come loose and drift around the cabin. Now, most of these so-called ideas are flotsam with no real value, but it's still a whole lot better than trying to squeeze something useful out of a conference room full of dummies in suits. At the end of the day, ideas make the world go round. A business is a living thing, and it takes a steady influx of ideas to keep the thing alive. That's what I'm doing on this plane. Hunting for ideas."

As I sit there unable to speak, Abrams takes the net between two fingers and brings it up to my face.

"The net's made of silver thread. Filigree. It's got a million spells woven into it, too small to see. It's one of a kind—handcrafted by an artisan in Afghanistan. Ideas tend to stay away from metal, but organic materials simply won't do the trick. Believe me, I sank plenty of time and money into net after net before discovering that silver thread is the ideal material for catching ideas. Silver repels evil, as anyone can tell you. That means bad ideas steer clear of the net and I don't have to worry about catching anything I don't want. Two birds, one stone, so to speak."

I glance at Abrams's triumphant expression, then at the net in his fingers, then at his face again, buying myself the time necessary to translate what he's just said. I tinker with his words, rearranging them while waiting patiently for the tiny dictionary in my head to tell me what they mean. Once I believe I've got the gist of the giant's prolix pronouncement, I put on a smile and respond:

"I think I understand. Maybe that's why it's so hard for me to read in the air."

Abrams furrows his brow. He brings his net-swooping to a sudden stop, looks me in the eye, then lifts his log-like arm and rests the silver net on my head.

"Why don't you tell me about that?"

There's nothing to tell. Personally, I find it impossible to read when I'm travelling. It's just the way I'm built. I can't concentrate. The words don't stick. But there's probably something behind that. And if there's some sort of mechanism at play, maybe a special kind of book could be produced to take advantage of that.

Abrams weighs what I've said in stilted English, then replies:

"Books... You're saying you can't read them?"

"That's what I'm saying."

"And not because you're an arm short?" he asks, his glance shifting to the book in my lap.

With the net still on my head, I look down at the book, too. *Untold Tales for Those with Three Arms*. I grabbed the paperback from a towering stack at the airport shop, where I learnt that the hardcover had been a bestseller, even though its true meaning is apparently lost on anyone unequipped with a tertiary arm—meaning it's nothing but dead weight to me.

"You don't read books?" I ask.

"No," Abrams responds with a proud snort. "First of all, they don't hold any practical value for me. I haven't touched a book since I finished high school—not that I was an avid reader back then. I don't have the time to invest in anything so impractical. If I ever found myself in a pinch and I absolutely needed to read a book, well, I'd hire someone to it for me. Rest assured, I'd never ask them to provide me with a summary of what they'd read. A book report by a third party has no value. As for the book itself, why should it mind who's doing the reading? So long as it gets read—that's all it takes for a book to do its job."

Perhaps deciding he's collected enough of our

conversation, Abrams removes the net from my head and goes on:

"Then again, if there's demand, that's a different story. Here I had you pegged as a big reader, but you say travel throws you for a loop, huh? So you're looking for a book that you can read while travelling..."

I nod.

"Moving around like this," I say, "I can never keep hold of my thoughts. It's like they fly off. I can't keep my mind on the book. All I see is ink. Time and place slip away, and I lose track of how it's all supposed to connect. I can't remember what came before, and what lies ahead starts looking like it's hidden in some kind of fog. When I'm on the train to work, I can manage, but I can't get anywhere if I'm on the shinkansen or the ICE. It's even worse on a plane, which makes me think it has something to do with speed. Travelling this fast, my thoughts can't keep up. Well, maybe those loose thoughts are the very ideas you're going around catching."

I point at the net that Abrams is once again absent-mindedly whisking through the air.

As we go on talking, it starts to click. Considering Abrams's unusual objective, there really is no better hunting ground than a commercial airliner. Large numbers of people strapped to their seats inside a container moving at high velocity, all their formless ideas breaking free and flying around the plane.

"So, how would one go about writing a book to be read when travelling?" Abrams asks as he leans towards me, the bulge of his belly spilling over the armrest between us.

I cock my head in response. If such a thing could be done, wouldn't someone have done it ages ago? But who knows, maybe the idea's simply slipped through the cracks. After all, serious readers despise books meant for specific purposes. Books to be given as gifts, books meant for sick friends, books to be read while doing a headstand, books to be read in transit, books for businesspeople. Books that don't even need to be read. Books that are actually best left unread. There's something about that degree of function that sucks all the fun out of it.

Just then, a thought tumbles out of my mouth: "It could be a translation."

"A translation," Abrams parrots back. "You mean taking a bestseller from some other part of the globe and turning it into your own language?"

"Not exactly. More like translating a book to fit a specific situation. Dostoevsky for people on the move. Pushkin for entrepreneurs..."

Hearing myself speak, I can tell I'm a little off the mark. I try to correct course: "Whatever it is, it would have to be tailored for that purpose."

I can see the cogs turning behind Abrams's large eyes.

"So, the book would have to be written under specific conditions? Say I hire a writer, then have him more or less live on a plane—along the lines of what I'm doing now. You think what that writer puts down on paper would hold up? Could you read something like that on the go?"

"Maybe... I'm not too sure," I say and leave it at that. The proposition is too absurd, too strange to entertain.

After all, if we start down that path, wouldn't that imply that a poet on the brink of death could write lines that would lead their audience into the afterlife? Or an impoverished novelist could pen a piece that would drag its readers into destitution? On one hand, that makes some sense to me; on the other, I know it isn't right. I can't think it through, though. Probably because we're flying through the air at high speed.

"Who knows what makes authors write the things they do in the first place..." I say, playing it safe.

"Well, that isn't very professional, is it?" Abrams said, sitting up in his seat, apparently enraged.

"Once they've agreed to do the job, it's the writer's responsibility to produce a work according to the specifications provided. That's what the contract is for. If the goal is to produce a book to be read in flight, we'll have to make sure it is indeed suitable for airplane reading. In fact, there ought to be some stipulation that at least thirty per cent of a randomly selected sample of passengers must be able to read the whole book, cover to cover."

Before my eyes, Abrams's bloated face is turning redder by the second. The image of a meatloaf smothered in tomato sauce appears in my mind, then vanishes. So this is how non-readers think. Somehow I doubt any author anywhere would be willing to sign a contract like that.

"But even if somebody read the whole book, that's no guarantee that they enjoyed it. If completability is your sole criterion, then the author would probably try to come up with something as short as possible... I mean, what's going to stop them from writing a one-word book?" I ask, doing my very best to play along.

Abrams's response leaves me utterly dumbfounded: "Well, what's the problem with that?"

*　*　*

A. A. Abrams. Born in Michigan in 1952.

Guided by an unconventional business philosophy, Abrams built up and sold off a wide variety of companies on his way to establishing a modest empire.

Early in his career, he made a small fortune with "Tiny Flyer Pacifiers"—a Manchu–Han imperial feast for babies. As the story goes, the idea came to him while he was on a flight, sitting a row or two away from a baby that screamed from take-off to touch-down. Each of Abrams's pacifiers offered a smorgasbord of fingernail-sized paste dabs that would take an infant diner a full day to make their way through. (Of course, the baby wouldn't finish the meal. Presented with this veritable feast of heavenly delights, they'd either doze off, overwhelmed and sated, or arrive at their destination before making it that far.) Needless to say, Abrams's creation enjoyed considerable popularity among exhausted mummies and daddies taking their fussy munchkins on lengthy trips.

This foray into the baby-food industry secured Abrams a permanent seat flying economy, but what allowed him to upgrade to business class was his sudden pivot into the world of publishing.

His breakthrough title was *To Be Read Only on an Airplane*, which, after a slow start, gained incredible momentum by word of mouth—among the well-off passengers of luxury liners. Airport sales were actually abysmal, but after a certain book critic found a long-forgotten copy of the book in their luggage while on a cruise, the title started making its way around with explosive speed. When bookshops back on land heard about this, they started promoting it as "The Luxury Liner Essential". And with that, the book flew off the shelves. The reviews that followed were underwhelming, but Abrams pushed back: "The book's true value can be grasped only when read on a luxury liner." Challenged in this way, people naturally had to find out for themselves if there was any truth to the businessman's claim. The stunt garnered even greater publicity for the book, landing it in the hands of even more curious consumers. Readers who managed to read all the way to the book's conclusion were few and far between, but this presumably made little difference to Abrams himself.

Abrams had hoped to catch lightning in a bottle twice; but his next effort, *To Be Read Only on a Luxury Liner*, was too on-the-nose and languished in obscurity for some time. The failure didn't deter Abrams, who continued to produce one flop after another: *To Be Read Only on a Commuter Train*, *To Be Read Only on the Uphill Walk to School*, etc. Some time later, the German translation of *To Be Read Only when Riding a Motorcycle*—Abrams's most uninspired title to date—was found to be ideal reading for passengers flying across the Pacific and climbed its way onto the bestseller list. In this way, the *To Be Read Only...* series found new life—as a sort of game in which people tried to determine where it was that certain editions of certain translations of certain titles in the series were in fact best read.

Abrams was famous primarily for his eccentric character and spent his later years almost entirely in flight. He adopted the silver butterfly net as his personal trademark, an image that can be found on every product manufactured by his various companies. Meanwhile, Abrams's own image appeared multiple times on the cover of industry magazines. In these photos, Abrams is almost always reclining in a first-class seat, a miniature net peeking out of his breast pocket like a silk handkerchief.

Abrams continued to pursue a wide array of projects, publicly insisting that each idea was one he'd captured in the cabin of a plane.

In one interview, Abrams was asked: "Using that butterfly net of yours to get conversations going with fellow flyers was a real stroke of brilliance. Where did you come up with that?"

His response couldn't have been any clearer: "No, you haven't been listening. This net can truly capture ideas."

"You mean objects get caught in it?"

(Well, of course they do. There's nothing strange about a net that catches things.)

"It was nineteen seventy-four. I was on a flight to Switzerland when I noticed that a butterfly had flown into the hat I was using to fan myself..."

"There was a butterfly on the plane?"

"No, no, you haven't been listening," Abrams replied indignantly. "I'm talking about ideas. This butterfly slipped right through my hat... Undeniable evidence that it wasn't of this world. At the same time, I could see it, so it had to be real. I knew I had to catch it."

Perhaps not wanting to agitate Abrams further, the interviewer quickly changed tack. While many businesspeople who enjoy enduring success harbour patently absurd beliefs to explain their great fortune, these are ultimately anecdotal and hardly likely to capture the interest of a serious, business-minded readership.

That being so, I'll pick up where that interview left off. During the remainder of our Seattle-bound flight, Abrams continued his tale, lowering his voice to a confidential whisper. Apparently practised at sharing the story with any party willing to hear him out, he spoke with all the colour and charm of a seasoned raconteur.

As he told it, the butterfly that flew through his hat was visible *only to him*. There he was, waving his hat at what appeared to be nothing at all, much to the dismay of the passengers seated around him. He was mere moments away from being escorted to the sickbay, but avoided this fate by asking for some sugar water. Warily, the flight attendant brought Abrams a cup of water with a couple of sugar cubes in it, and soon after the imaginary butterfly that had until then eluded capture fluttered over to alight on the glass. Abrams covered the glass with his hat, at which point the butterfly must have gone to sleep.

It was nothing short of a miracle, Abrams told me, that he was able to transport the sleeping specimen to the Montreux Palace Hotel, where he had it examined by a lepidopterist who happened to be staying there.

"This is an imaginary butterfly," the lepidopterist said as soon as he laid eyes on the insect resting on the rim of the glass. Abrams, who'd suspected as much all along, said nothing.

"A new species, and an imaginary one at that. The female."

In what had to have been an attempt to disguise his incredible excitement, the lepidopterist started muttering something, not that Abrams caught a single word of it. He watched as the man quickly reached out to take the butterfly between his fingers.

To Abrams, this seemed as natural as the lepidopterist's ability to see the imaginary butterfly in the first place.

The butterfly's abdomen was striped in four bands of colour: blue, red, purple and black, in descending order. Her wings were gridded with black lines, the squares filled in with white, red, blue, green, yellow, orange and purple, arranged in a playful pattern.

This pattern was visible only when the butterfly's wings were closed. Or in brief flashes when she was in flight.

"She's the perfect picture of a harlequin."

With obvious satisfaction, the lepidopterist paused as he stroked his chin, then announced: "Arlequinus arlequinus."

He smiled at Abrams, who stood there with a puzzled look on his face.

"Her Latin binomial."

"... And that's where I got the name," the man said as he held out his massive hand to shake mine. "A. A. Abrams, at your service."

II

THERE YOU HAVE IT: THE NEAR-COMPLETE TRANSLATION OF 'To Be Read Only under a Cat', by the extraordinary polyglot writer Tomoyuki Tomoyuki. As the translation is my own, it's safe to assume that the stylistic effect often credited to the original has been all but lost here. And, beyond style, I cannot say with any confidence that I've even managed to convey the work's fundamental meaning. 'Under a Cat' is written in *Latino sine flexione*. While Tomoyuki Tomoyuki has produced an incredible amount of work across dozens of languages, presumably acquired over the course of the author's many travels, 'Under A Cat' is the only piece we have in this auxiliary language.

The brainchild of Italian mathematician Giuseppe Peano, *Latino sine flexione* is a language best understood as classical Latin disembarrassed of its inflections. As this language never had many speakers—no more than a handful of enthusiasts, really—there isn't an established body of writing to reference, and I often had to rely on instinct when working on this translation. Needless to say, when the author strayed from what might be called standard usage, resorting to what appears to be slang or idiom, or putting the books away and winging it, I had nowhere to turn for assistance to get to the heart of the text.

For my translation, I used the facsimile edition of the story held in the A. A. Abrams Collection.

On the double name Tomoyuki Tomoyuki, there are numerous theories, but one thing can be said with certainty: it's extremely unlikely that Tomoyuki Tomoyuki is the author's real name. Witnesses at multiple sites claim to have seen an Asian man—probably Japanese, Chinese or Korean—entering and exiting an apartment believed to be occupied by the author. Among the myriad works currently attributed to this enigmatic figure, only one has been signed with an East Asian name; thus, for the sake of convenience, it is by this moniker that the author is known.

We have very little concrete information about the life of Tomoyuki Tomoyuki. Yet even in the absence of the artist himself, unpublished works believed to have been written by Tomoyuki Tomoyuki have been discovered in large number. To date, the author's writings have been found at more than thirty locations globally. This being so, he may be regarded as something of an outlier—even within the world of outsider art.

At every site, the author appears to use only the local language, continuing his writing in secret. With each new language, he also changes the name with which he signs his work. It was a man in the employ of one A. A. Abrams who first postulated that this massive body of work had in fact originated from a single hand.

It all began when Abrams—a businesswoman who had broken into real estate—had a rent collector enter the abandoned unit of a tenant who had fallen into arrears. In the room, the collector discovered a treasure trove of materials and tools: spools of silver and copper wire, pliers, soldering irons, scissors, needles, thread, mounds of yarn, metal clay, glue, origami paper, et cetera, et cetera. He also found a large amount of hand-written work rivalling the towering piles of odds and ends.

Picking up on the scent of potential profit, Abrams decided to commit significant capital and manpower to the pursuit of the missing individual. A detailed account of this border-crossing game of hide-and-seek can be found in 'The Fugue of Tomoyuki Tomoyuki', the final chapter of Abrams's unfinished autobiography.

Abrams's pursuit of the ever-elusive Tomoyuki Tomoyuki eventually ended in failure, and no substantial leads regarding the author's whereabouts have turned up since. Apparently the author had caught on to the fact that Abrams had caught on to *him*—at which point he slyly placed one final piece atop the pile of pages: 'To Be Read Only under a Cat'.

So: what did it mean for Tomoyuki Tomoyuki to write this piece in Latin, a language presently used by virtually no one? And why did he opt for a simplified version of the language developed by a twentieth-century mathematician? Theories abound. As Tomoyuki Tomoyuki typically writes in the language of wherever he is at the time, and considering the fact that A. A. Abrams makes an explicit appearance in 'Under a Cat', popular opinion is that the decision to write in *Latino sine flexione* must represent some kind of knowing wink on the part of the author.

Many believe that Tomoyuki Tomoyuki was effectively casting his pursuer in the role of Arlecchino and announcing that this globe-spanning chase would be continued in another realm: one under the dominion of a dead tongue. To accept this interpretation is to view 'Under a Cat' as a grave malediction. While it wouldn't have been all that strange for the piece to have been written in Latin, merely a dead language, this was *Latino sine flexione*: a dead language fashioned from yet another dead language.

The notion that the author was extending a cursed invitation to his pursuer is a haunting one indeed.

Of course, what has drawn many to this idea is the fact that, shortly after procuring this purportedly accursed work, A. A. Abrams did leave this plane of existence—dying in flight, no less. In other words, there are those who believe that 'Under a Cat' was meant for an audience of exactly one: Abrams herself. They believe that this text was responsible for the mogul's untimely demise.

Needless to say, this romantic reading has a certain appeal, but we have more than enough evidence to disprove it.

First of all, A. A. Abrams had been diagnosed with uterine cancer several years prior to her death.

In addition, Abrams's cause of death was determined to be deep-vein thrombosis, otherwise known as "economy-class syndrome": an utterly unsurprising outcome, given her long history of stuffing herself into unforgiving airliner seats.

Finally—and this is the decisive blow—Abrams was never known to be a reader. On this point alone can

Tomoyuki Tomoyuki's liberty-laden tale be considered a faithful portrayal of reality. (We likely need to chalk this up to coincidence as the two never crossed paths.) As "a mogul's mogul", Abrams readily broadcast the fact that she had no interest in reading books. And in this case, with a text written in an obscure language, it seems even less likely that she would have attempted to engage with the work in question.

No one can say with any degree of certainty what it was that Tomoyuki Tomoyuki had in mind when he wrote 'Under a Cat', but—if I may venture a guess of my own—it appears to be little more than a record reflecting the author's state of mind at the time. Needless to say, there are various ways in which we can understand Tomoyuki Tomoyuki's language choice without suggesting that 'Under a Cat' was deployed as a supernatural murder weapon.

It would make perfect sense for the itinerant author, presumably exhausted by learning new languages with every move, to turn to an interlingua aimed at meeting the language needs of multiple communities. But the fact that Tomoyuki Tomoyuki wrote only one work in *Latino sine flexione* would seem to suggest that the author had some reason to give up on the language after writing 'Under a Cat'.

There's one more theory of note. While this may seem more than a little outlandish, it is nonetheless possible that, when Tomoyuki Tomoyuki wrote 'Under a Cat', he was in the company of people using *Latino sine flexione* in their daily lives.

As a variation on this idea, it's conceivable that Tomoyuki Tomoyuki was actually residing in a domain of dead language at the time. Then again, as this particular story was found in the garret of an old inn in Mistas, among a number of works written in Ndyuka, this idea has very few supporters. Mistas was, and continues to be, a truly vibrant city—not what one would expect from a lifeless necropolis.

The fact that *Latino sine flexione* was developed by a mathematician has also led some to pay attention to the piece's mathematical properties. In fact, this was how I first caught on to Tomoyuki Tomoyuki myself. As far-fetched as it may sound, the idea that 'Under a Cat' could be a mathematical theorem disguised as a literary work is certainly an intriguing one. And yet there's nothing in the structure of Peano's revised Latin that makes it particularly suited to the expression of mathematical content. The language was primarily designed to keep things as simple as possible—to trim away Latin's onerous conjugations and agreements.

Given this, there's little to be gained from a mathematically minded reading of 'Under a Cat'. Once I realized this to be the case, my interest shifted to Tomoyuki Tomoyuki's life and the work itself.

'To Be Read Only under a Cat' cannot be found in *The Selected Writings Of Tomoyuki Tomoyuki*. The total volume of work produced by the author is astounding. To date, less than one per cent of it has appeared in translation. Even the pieces included in *The Selected Writings* are just that: *pieces*. But what else could the editors have done? Most of Tomoyuki Tomoyuki's work is fragmentary and incomplete, with much of it having been scribbled down on scraps of paper with no discernible flow or order, even though many of them appear to be numbered sequentially.

Tomoyuki Tomoyuki's *oeuvre* can certainly be described as a mixed bag, and perhaps it will be some time before we can determine whether 'Under a Cat' is in fact a gem or an ordinary rock. A relatively recent find (the story was discovered after the compilation of *The Selected Writings*), this work is only the latest by Tomoyuki Tomoyuki to enjoy its fifteen minutes of fame. Of course, the idea that the story is cursed has helped to attract an additional degree of interest. As continued research leads to further discoveries, these too will have their moment in the sun—only to return to the shade before long.

Sometimes I'm tempted to think of Tomoyuki Tomoyuki's entire body of work as some sort of gigantic machine kept in motion by constant discovery.

At present, most scholars of Tomoyuki Tomoyuki's work focus on comparing different passages from various texts. New translations of his work are regrettably rare, and with that in mind I'm honoured to be able to share my translation of 'To Be Read Only under a Cat' in its near-complete state.

Tomoyuki Tomoyuki. Year of birth unknown. Place of birth unknown. Whether the author is dead or alive—also not known.

As he moves from hotel room to row house, the author leaves prodigious amounts of writing in his wake, but even now the true scope of his output remains a mystery. Tomoyuki Tomoyuki is believed to have produced a body of writing close to the equivalent of 200,000 pages of A4 paper, yet any attempt to truly apprehend Tomoyuki Tomoyuki's work is complicated by the fact that he has written in a wide range of languages and scripts. The author is thought to have made use of about thirty languages during different stages in his life, but this is only an estimate. Should we decide to distinguish between various dialects, one study suggests, then the number of languages quickly approaches triple digits.

It's believed that our species has the capacity to make use of up to twenty different languages. The famed polyglot Heinrich Schliemann is thought to have used a number close to that, and is said to have achieved fluency in around fifteen of them. (Then again, a number of those languages—English, German, French, etc.—are deeply intertwined. According to Pliny the Elder, King Mithridates VI of Pontus spoke all twenty-two languages found within his dominion; to be sure, in the past, members of the educated class were often familiar with the languages of neighbouring societies, and this could perhaps be viewed as an extreme example of that phenomenon.)

Yet Tomoyuki Tomoyuki has produced work in at least twenty different language *families*. This means that, in his writing, we find a number of languages with different writing systems, lexical roots, and grammatical structures.

While on the surface this may strike us as superhuman, it is not entirely without precedent. Daniel Tammet, for example, who has command of fifteen languages, is widely known for his exceptional linguistic abilities. Again, this number alone is not terribly rare, but what sets Tammet apart from other polyglots is the speed with which he can acquire a new tongue. Starting from nothing, he managed to master Icelandic in just one week.

Tomoyuki Tomoyuki's linguistic ability can only be described as preternatural.

It's one thing to speak multiple languages and to be able to use them to get your ideas across in the moment, but it's another thing entirely to be able to express yourself in written form, pinning your ideas down in time and place. Writing is an acquired skill—apparently unnecessary for our survival, it's not something we're naturally equipped with as hominids.

The handwritten work attributed to Tomoyuki Tomoyuki has been subjected to numerous types of scrutiny, and the results support the idea that we are dealing with a single author making use of multiple languages and multiple pen names. There are those who posit the existence of a secret society that has collectively continued the author's work, mimicking his penmanship to a T, but fingerprint analysis has recently put such arguments to rest. While it's possible to imagine (especially for those of us who are fond of detective novels) ream upon ream of paper being marked with identical sets of fingerprints and distributed to various locations around the globe, the sheer number of pages left behind makes this scenario seem all but unthinkable.

At the same time, it has already been established that some portion of Tomoyuki Tomoyuki's output is simply copied work. "Work" may in fact be a stretch: many of these lines are borrowed from ads, popular songs and other ephemera. It appears as though the author produced an omnium gatherum of whatever caught his eye and entered his ear. Among his work, we sometimes find sequences that start out as little more than noise—a slapdash hotchpotch of different styles and registers—but eventually coalesce into a single voice.

It can be oddly moving to witness this process as it unfolds, and yet the power of that feeling quickly fades when you realize that the author has produced a staggering amount of work that follows the same pattern.

What does it mean for someone to leave behind a "staggering" amount of work documenting the process of learning a language from beginning to end? Could it actually be that Tomoyuki Tomoyuki starts the process over every time he completes a given work?

One camp of developmental linguists, who initially assumed that these pieces were evidence of his language acquisition process, tried to salvage their value as primary material by proposing that the author is composing multiple texts in parallel. In other words, they suggest, he takes multiple sheets of paper and produces one line on each one before moving on to the next.

Judging from the work he's left behind, Tomoyuki Tomoyuki stays in a given place for no more than one year—neither settling down nor simply passing through—and this makes it very difficult to determine the order in which the author's works have been created. While some of his writings contain dates, they cannot be taken at face value. After all, even in Tomoyuki Tomoyuki's seemingly autobiographical writings, we often encounter events that appear to have occurred after the death of the person understood to be writing the work. Age and gender also vary with remarkable frequency. Some have proposed the use of ink analysis to establish the order in which Tomoyuki Tomoyuki's writings have been authored, but as the writer is known to change pens at the drop of a hat—in extreme cases, doing so in the middle of a single word—such analysis would presumably not shed any new light on the situation.

There's little evidence upon which any judgments can be made.

Scratches, smears, fingerprints on the page, fold lines in the paper. Based on the data gained from the practically Sisyphean task of cataloguing these elements, it seems highly likely that Tomoyuki Tomoyuki wrote each piece independently.

Of course, we can bypass this maelstrom of unknowns if we simply subscribe to the notion that Tomoyuki Tomoyuki is a writer who possesses the ability to mimic the acquisition of language itself.

He acts out the acquisition of a language, repeating the process over and over. From the outside, it appears effortless—so much so that it feels contrived. Yet Tomoyuki Tomoyuki continues to use the language of that place *exclusively*. With the abilities that we believe Tomoyuki Tomoyuki to possess, it would seem reasonable for him to produce stories that use multiple languages—or maybe even to develop a language of his own—but nowhere can we find such phenomena among his writings. While we often find chaotic beginnings in Tomoyuki Tomoyuki's work, these inevitably turn out to be nothing more than transcriptions of sound clumsily written in the local script while clinging to the grammar of the language of the place where he stayed last.

The extraordinary focus required to produce an unthinkable quantity of work. The lack of attachment to any language in particular. An approach that almost makes it seem as if he's working in order to forget the language that came before. At a certain point, it's only logical to consider the possibility of a cognitive anomaly—that a fundamentally different function is taking place within the author's brain.

Once we arrive here, we have to ask: is language the same thing for Tomoyuki Tomoyuki as it is for the rest of us? It almost seems as though he's some sort of vessel into which language has been poured. That's not how language normally works. Generally speaking, you need tools if you're going to build a structure. So, faced with such a structure, we can only assume that the necessary tools were used in its making. But what if that isn't true? What if Tomoyuki Tomoyuki has access to all languages and remembers the specifics of a given one only when returning to it?

While few in number, there are some passages among the author's writings that could perhaps serve to illuminate his own thoughts on language learning.

When I write, I begin with the A-B-C song. Every language has one. Otherwise I can start with the 1-2-3s. Or the do-re-mi song. But that one can be unsettling. Not all scales have the same number of notes. I can't write something down if it doesn't have a name. As I look around to see where the thing that I thought had a name has gone, my pen hovers, if only for the briefest moment. Before long, I forget what it was I was looking for, then lose track of what I was trying to write in the first place. Much like how I can't make sense of what I've written in the past unless I'm back in that place. Like how these lines I'm putting down now will end up lost beneath piles of writing. Time follows the same rules as space.

A pivot, a set phrase. A sequence of words to get you from here to there. This one takes the form of a door. A narrow opening—no other way in. Why does it flow the way it does? Something makes me hesitate. Because, while I am certain there's an entrance here, there's no possible way of knowing if an exit exists.

That's the wrong way to use this word, they tell me. It can't be used like that. I can't see the reason for it, but if that's how it is then that's how it is. My solution is simple enough. Never use the word again. Not using the word is my choice. There aren't that many words that can't be worked around. But I wonder. What if I come across a language out there where every word rubs me the wrong way? Then how would I write? What if there's a language out there where every sentence structure feels wrong? Could I even enter a place like that?

There you have it. And so it is. It is what it certainly is. Now again as it always was. Just as exactly as I always thought. Perhaps in the end no more than ever. And there you have it. If not for the sound of these words, I wouldn't have written any of this. But what's the sound doing here? Why is it allowed to exist? How can it take over the way it does, latching on to me, making me write things I wasn't even thinking?

The above are excerpts from Tomoyuki Tomoyuki's diaristic writings—words that would seem to belong to the author himself, or perhaps another person who may have happened to be present.

When it comes to Tomoyuki Tomoyuki, one can never run out of things to talk about.

For instance, a group of story fragments written in various languages—the writing at times flowing, at others halting. The pieces share the same title, but there appears to be no connection between them in terms of plot or content.

Or perhaps I ought to mention the tale of the river-crossing Indian that frequently appears in Tomoyuki Tomoyuki's work. It features a plot that is notoriously difficult to remember. For this reason, it's often used in experiments designed to test memory. As I'm currently away from home and don't have the text with me, I cannot offer even a basic summary of the episode. While this work is often cited as evidence of Tomoyuki Tomoyuki's superhuman recall, it's certainly possible that the writer is simply carrying his notes for the story with him every time he moves.

When it comes to what we know—or *think* we know—about the author of 'Under a Cat', we always find ourselves back in the same place: trapped in a tangled mess of hypotheses and counter-hypotheses that make it impossible to claim to know anything at all. There was a time when the entire field was under the impression that Tomoyuki Tomoyuki had indeed invented a language of his own. It was all they could talk about, too—until it was discovered that the language in question was actually a type of pidgin English: a variation spoken by the old women of a certain locale. The language is one of several found in this region, where different language communities had been broken up by the state and made to settle in a sort of mosaic pattern to keep them from consolidating power.

Among Tomoyuki Tomoyuki's writings, we've also come across fragments of languages that have only recently gone extinct.

Even at this moment, additional work by Tomoyuki Tomoyuki is surely out there somewhere—waiting impatiently to be discovered.

I began this essay with the words "There you have it"—as an homage of sorts to the author. My only hope is that I've managed to follow these words in the right direction.

THERE'S SOMETHING SIMILAR ABOUT KITCHENS AND dictionaries.

You can feel it when you're done cooking and mulling over the day's meals, your thoughts returning to the food you still have and what you have to buy on your next trip to the market. It's in the way you're always missing something and need to make do with what you have, the way there are no wrong combinations—or right ones.

But with a little effort, you get where you're going.

Coriander, cumin, cardamom, mint, paprika, raisins, tomatoes, onions, olives, almonds, pistachios, yogurt, mutton, couscous. That's what the kitchen has for me today. I bought too much coriander, so my fridge is going to have to revolve around that for a while. The ingredients I can't use up today will shape tomorrow's menu, as determined by what will go bad when. Whatever the dish, my pointy-headed tajine will make short work of it.

Words swirl around inside my head.

Coriander, cilantro, phak chi, and Chinese parsley all somehow refer to the same plant.

Word after word starts to form—in Standard Arabic, in French, in Spanish, in Tashelhit, in Tasusit, in Tarifit, in Moroccan Arabic. They make it as far as my throat, but never complete the trip. Or the words arrive—but by then they've been replaced with other words. No matter what you call it, every apple is a local one, wrapped up in the exotic sound of another place.

The simple act of thinking about stalks of coriander seems to bring up so many things, all at once, its many names changing everything from the smell to the shade of green. Each sound calls up a fragrant mouthful. The scent brings an air with it and the air summons a town; where there's a town there are people, and where there are people you'll find the bustle of life.

The old city of Fez is one of the world's great maze cities. Cars are turned away at the Blue Gate, and as you make your way through the narrow lanes choked with people and horses, everything emerges suddenly and without context—as if in a mosaic. Turn at the corner shop with the birdcages hanging outside and you'll come across a butcher's stall, beside it a communal well, and then a spot where you're assaulted by the smell of ammonia from the tannery when the wind blows in a certain direction. An endless parade of decorations dangling from the eaves, spices paddled into spiky cones that almost look like gelato, the little legs of children dancing briskly as they carry dough towards the communal oven.

Fez. Fes. Fas. An ideal city for anyone who needs to disappear for a little while. The sound has yet to settle inside me.

Streets criss-cross other streets, forming a web, so you can never be sure which street you're on. Roads that don't appear on the map, roads that don't match up with the ones listed. People call it a maze, but live here and at some point the streets simply become streets. Like the branching paths of a cave system: a baffling labyrinth from the mouth, but a clear-cut path out from the inside.

Tarz fassi—a form of embroidery practised in this old capital for centuries is a backstitch that creates the same pattern on both sides of a fabric. I'm here to learn how it works, to bring it into myself. From the street, I glimpse women sitting in a dim room, stitching fine designs into pieces of cloth stretched over wooden frames. While some might see this as simply another reversible stitch, the details are, of course, unique. You count the threads in the cloth as you go, which means the level of meticulousness is extreme; progress is almost imperceptible. You embroider the geometric arabesques directly onto the cloth with no visible guide to go by.

I'm sure the definitive text describing this technique is out there somewhere, but I'm not so interested in that. You don't need knowledge of geometry to produce geometric patterns. So long as the body moves first, there's no need to bring your head into it. Just let your fingers do the talking.

I've become close with a wizened old woman who sits in a rattan chair set up right outside her workshop, fingers in motion all day long. When she sees me coming, she offers me a seat. She doesn't talk about anything in particular, but her hands speak volumes.

When I first arrived, crowds would gather around us. They took me for a hapless eccentric there only to learn to embroider, incapable of anything else. Now they leave us be. I suppose they eventually decided there was no cause for concern. The people here could hardly be warmer. They're always ready to share kitchen tips even though I'm not asking. Gatherings spark discussions, and the commotion attracts even more people, leading to even larger conversations. Which herbs to put in the tajine, in what quantity and when. How many cardamom pods to add to the coffee, how to crush them. Where to go to find the best desert roses. What to mix into the dye to get a better yellow. One topic brings up another, the conversation expanding, twisting and turning until the day is over.

Once people got used to seeing me around, they joked that my face was starting to look like one of theirs. While I hadn't blended in completely, they'd come to see me as some sort of foreign fixture set up outside the shop. When passers-by would ask the shopkeeper about me, he'd nod. Oh, them? They're here to learn how to stitch from my mother. How'd that happen? Well, funny you should ask... I can imagine the conversation unfolding between them. When someone tries to talk to me, he steps in and calls them away. It's kind of funny how he's appointed himself my protector.

Learning a stitch is easier than learning to spell its name. Because the thing is actually there in front of you.

I came to this place with no words at all. With a faltering hello, I opened my bag, took out my tools, and showed the woman my handiwork: flowing lines embroidered on black cloth in Holbein stitch.

The woman takes it from me with a suspicious look on her face, then flips it over to find the same pattern on the other side. She thinks for a while, tracing the ridges of the stitches with her fingers, then removes a piece of needlework from the pouch at her side and hands it to me. Checking the front and back, I count the stitches off on my fingers, then flip the piece over in my mind. She offers me a needle and some cloth in a wooden frame. I take it, work two stitches forward, then take a second thread to work two stitches back. Having created a line four stitches long, I slowly turn the frame over so she can see. I hand it to her and she picks up where I left off, working one stitch forward and one stitch back. Then she smiles and nods in understanding.

She pulls out a chair and pats the seat. Come sit, come sit.

Even as she continues her Fez stitch, she spins up an unbroken string of words. She works on both sides of the fabric, and yet her eyes stay fixed to the front, never bothering to check the opposite side. Her needle moves with practised speed, but the pattern's so fine that, as I watch, I can't help feeling like time is standing still.

You know, this was all women ever did in the old days. Girls had to stay in and sew. When you finished your sewing, you could do whatever you wanted, but—funny thing—there was no finishing it, no matter how you kept at it. Well, I suppose you've already figured that out for yourself, haven't you? It can take a year or two to finish a single bedspread.

I'm sure she's saying something like that. The words she speaks are more than words. They're a kind of ritual—the kind that accompanies any kind of handwork. People say the same things all over the world. So much so you don't really need the language to understand what it is that's being said. I keep my eyes on the woman's hands as I turn my ear to her words. I know what she's saying, even if I don't know what the sounds mean. When I repeat back what I hear, the old woman's hands come to a sudden stop.

Oh my, oh my.

Her eyes open wide among the sea of wrinkles.

Oh my. Looks like I need to teach you the language, too, don't I?

Oh my. Looks like I need to teach you the language, too, don't I?

I copy her every sound. We smile.

"Where in the world did you come from?"

"I don't know. But I have four passports."

Mimicking each sound she makes to the best of my ability, I convey something completely different in return. I reach into my bag and pull out my passports.

"I see. Four passports."

She scrutinizes my documents as if it were her job. I repeat her words right back to her:

"I see. Four passports."

The woman stares intently at my lips, almost as if she's trying to learn *my* language. Opening her mouth wide and speaking as slowly as she can, she corrects my pronunciation and grammar.

"Here are four passports."

"Here are four passports."

I take one back, cock my head, and wait silently for the words to come.

"Three passports."

"Three passports," I repeat.

When I grab a second passport, the woman pushes the other two back into my hands, then starts to sing. The counting song... Or is it the alphabet song? I can't tell the difference yet. As she sings, she returns to her stitching. My eyes on her fingers, I repeat every sound she makes. The tune goes on, working through its minor variations, asking me:

"What brought you here?"

"The Fez stitch did," I say using the same sounds.

"Tarz fassi takes a lot of time. It takes a long time to complete a piece, of course, but it takes years just to get the feel of it. It's something you start as a child. It's a lot to ask of an adult."

"There are plenty of techniques around the world that produce the same pattern on both sides. But lately I've been wondering: what if you could have a different pattern on either side? Separate designs would be one way to do it, but I feel like that's not the only way. There has to be some kind of convention or rule, a principle, and I thought it'd be faster to figure it out with my body than with my head. Plus, I had to leave town..."

Slowly, we keep up our impossible conversation using the same sounds.

Crafts are my passion, but they're really much more than that—they're how I make my living. I can't say for sure how long I've been doing this. Ever since I was born, really. But I can't stick to any particular craft long enough to become good at it; I put them down as soon as I pick them up. I'm always on the move, always starting something new. Fortunately, I'm decent with my hands, so I can earn enough to stay afloat, to move on. And when I don't have enough money to make my next move, I stay where I am until I do.

Why am I always so quick to move on? Maybe it's because there are certain things I can just see. What those things are, I'd rather not put into words. You could call them principles, or laws, but that doesn't describe my experience. I know it's not the monotony of repetition—after all, repetition is hardly monotonous. Even when what you're doing stays the same, the air around you is changing moment by moment. Even if Holbein and Fez are materially identical stitches, that doesn't mean they're the same thing. Every stitch, every seam has a sound of its own. I hate to think of myself as someone who gets bored easily, someone who scratches the surface and feels like I have it all figured out—satisfied by the work I've completed in my head.

But inevitably my body starts to carry me, moving of its own accord. My feet take me someplace new.

When I move on, it's never out of impulsiveness. That's the thing that keeps me in one place.

It's precarious to stake your livelihood on wares that are amateur at best, so I sell foreign traditions and materials instead. It's a modest trade, to say the least, but it's enough to make ends meet. When the concepts are exotic, even rudimentary work has value. I'll dabble in thread, sometimes clay. I'll spend a month spinning wool or blowing glass. But what I sell isn't the work, it's how the work is made. On rare occasions, I've transported more dangerous items—goods entirely unrelated to handicraft—but only when I'm in a bind.

As a rule, I live alone. I don't chase after those who leave, and I avoid those who come around. Sometimes I seek the company of others, but I never stay long. I often forget who I was with the day before, which has sometimes led to people walking away in exasperation. I've known men and women kind enough to ask me to come back and see them again, but I forget who they were the minute I step out the door.

When I'm doing my work, I'm almost never at home—I'm at a café, or a workshop, or on the move. I'll do only the lightest bit of practice where I'm staying. At night, I mostly write—by lamplight, by flashlight, by candlelight, by starlight, by no light at all. Every now and then, I put together a how-to book to earn a little money. Sometimes I'll take the manuscript to a local press, other times I'll mimeograph a few dozen copies myself. It's pointless to publish a book on a craft from the place where I am—there's always someone better qualified to do that—so I do the writing after I've moved on. In fact, I was only able to make a reliable living this way once a market for handicraft books had developed in Western Europe. You don't see much of it, but the market is actually enormous. Just like the work itself, it goes on and on, quietly and steadily expanding.

I learn the language at the same time as the craft, so my vocabulary tends to be well stocked with words related to handicrafts and cooking. Then I add dashes of whatever's lacking to the mix, the language knitted up row by row and simmered over time. My palate isn't sophisticated enough for me to set my sights on writing a cookbook.

I spend my nights writing. Most of what I write down is just sounds—I copy them down as I've heard them. When I do this, I'm not thinking. I doubt I could, even if I wanted to.

Oh my, oh my. My, my, my. My writing gets adjusted, my mistakes corrected. We don't write this way here. So I'm told from time to time. Usually, I do as I'm told, but there are some words and constructions that I can't abide. That's no good, I'm told—but I don't like coconut milk, I say back. Anyone who knows their way around a kitchen will smile in response, while those who keep to the living room will look at me with doubt.

Right around the time I've collected the necessary spices, I write an innocuous little story. I write down something I've heard, more or less the way I heard it.

I never intend for anyone to read what I write, and the content doesn't stick with me for long. It's not even my story to begin with. And that's why, when the time comes to put a name on it, I use the name of the person who's been teaching me their craft. I put these stories in writing to amuse myself, but every now and then they make someone smile. Strangely enough, no one's ever complained that it didn't sound like something they'd write.

Then, after a year at most, but usually after a few weeks, or sometimes a few hours, I move on.

Out of nowhere, it comes to me. The concept for some kind of craft. I know these ideas are rarely if ever new, so I look into it, and if it's already out there, I head to the place where I can learn it; sometimes I end up going back to a place I've been before, to remember a technique I've forgotten. I feel like I often end up starting over from square one—to make sure I've got the air just right, that I haven't missed any of the details.

I say "I feel like" because I don't actually remember.

Where was I living? What did I learn there? From whom? Those memories are gone. At a minimum, I can't find them now. Even though I was sure I'd never been to this town before, I feel something like déjà vu. Here we are again, I say to myself, and leave the rest to my legs. Without fail, they guide me someplace—to a key left on a window sill, or inside a flowerpot, or beneath a mat. The door opens. I step into the room and look over the writings piled high on the desk or the floor—words I'd left behind at some point in the past. Most of the time, I can't decipher the words, but I read them as I see them. I definitely recognize the handwriting, and I recognize the furniture, too. I nibble on some herb drying in the kitchen to confirm my current location. When I spot a bank in town, I reach into my bag and pull out bank card after bank card until I find one that works.

On every card, a different name.

This is how I remember. Because what I forget isn't the memories. It's where I've kept them.

As I remember, I repeat. I have no recollection of having been in this situation before, but the stacks of paper in front of me are all the proof I need. These things were written at some point in time, though I can't say if that was in the past or in the future. Then I start writing again—from the beginning. From the sound. I learn to write, learn to count—the words break down and come together, the flour forms little clumps, the lemon juice curdles the milk, the minced meat starts to stick, and the onion caramelizes in the pan.

Counting the threads, the stitches, the knots, I trace pattern after pattern onto the cloth.

I produce patterns—geometric, algebraic, differential—without knowing what they are. The patterns themselves have no meaning; the meaning is drawn from the pattern. In thread, in wire, in pencil, in ballpoint pen, in fountain pen, in silverpoint, I stitch the letters so the scripts I write appear the same on the back as they do on the front. So they aren't mirror images.

Then I turn that process into words. I capture the works in progress in photos for my books. I lose track of what I'm supposed to be doing. I start to feel like I'm not working towards a finished product at all, but only creating works in progress. And often that's true. Words, sentences abandoned before completion. These fragments make up my body of work—which is why my work is never complete. There's no end to it. Embroidery that begins as rug-weaving becomes knitting. A lace edging calls for beads, and those beads take the form of a flower that attracts a brass-wire butterfly.

The chain of creation goes on and on. Its form is constantly changing, cycling through the stages of transformation, setting new life in motion.

* * *

This happens in the air, between Tokyo and Seattle.

Mid-story, I find myself on a plane. Out of the corner of my eye, I'm watching two women across the aisle, their four hands moving this way and that as they speak. The tatting shuttle I have in my left hand passes under a span of silk pulled taut between my right thumb and middle finger then loops back over, again and again. You can't bring knitting needles or sewing needles on a plane, but the tatting shuttle, which holds the thread ahead in time instead of behind, is one of my favourite tools.

One of the women pulls a silver handkerchief from her chest pocket. No—what I thought was a handkerchief turns out to be a tiny bag wrapped around a small stick. And what seemed like silk is actually fine, incredibly fine silver thread. The egg in my mind hatches into a sterling-silver caterpillar, which spins itself into a silken cocoon. From that sheath emerges a brightly coloured butterfly that flutters around the cabin. The woman opens the bag.

A miniature butterfly net. Silver filigree.

"This net captures good luck," I hear her say. "I fell in love with it the second I saw it at the antique shop. They told me it wasn't for sale, but I kept going back until they changed their tune. It's got a billion spells woven into it, so tiny you can't even see them."

Yes, there are words woven into the net. But they aren't written out in letters you can read. The threads cross and tangle, the words flitting forward then turning back on themselves, capturing connections that wouldn't otherwise exist. That's their magic. I have no memory of the net the woman is holding, but its function is immediately apparent to me.

It doesn't catch luck. It catches opportunity.

It captures things that can only exist mid-journey, things that set the next leg of the journey in motion. It scoops up ideas left behind by the moving body—ideas that would otherwise vanish.

I've already forgotten all about it, but I'm sure that I created a net just like that one at some point. No, that isn't quite right, I realize. I'm going to create *that* net. In the future.

In that moment, there's no doubt in my mind.

Someone in the past collects that net from a room I abandon in the future. That's how it finds its way to the antique shop. The woman with the net operates an assortment of businesses, and, as part of her charity work, she offers low-cost housing to people without the necessary papers or permission to work. One of these rooms is mine. When I fail to pay my rent, one of her employees enters my room, finds the precious net and, considering it fair game, pockets it, then sells it to the antique shop for a song. There, Abrams finds the net, none the wiser to its provenance. Once she gets her hands on it, she lives out the rest of her days in the air—on one plane or another.

When the passenger in the next seat starts talking about a story that can be read only when travelling, the businesswoman captures it with her net. All the while thinking, "Where have I read that before?"

Abrams is a philanthropist, the sort of person who gives as much thought to the environment as to her own well-being. She's a huge bookworm, too, but for whatever reason she opts to keep that information private.

The story comes back to her.

It gives her an idea: why not take the work of mine she's discovered and share it with the world? Maybe there's a perfect time and place for reading what I wrote. If so, she can use her resources to make sure that my work gets where it needs to go. She feels a little guilty publishing someone else's work without their permission, but she tells herself the author would only benefit from the support.

This is how the story I'm hearing right now, *Untold Tales for Those with Three Arms*, comes to see the light of day—except no one in this world has three arms, so it stands no chance of being truly understood. It was originally a monologue on patterns that can only be created through the simultaneous use of three knitting needles, the kind of thing that fascinated me at some point. Of course, the answer to that particular riddle is simple enough. With a partner, someone on the same page, it's possible for two people to knit a single piece together, and in that case you've even got an arm to spare. It's that extra arm that writes *Untold Tales for Those with Three Arms*—a piece for three needles.

On a street corner somewhere, we're sitting face to face.

Or maybe there are three of us, each contributing one arm, working together to knit an otherwise impossible pattern.

For a net to catch miracles, it has to be the product of a miracle to begin with.

IV

IT'S MAY, AND I'M IN SAN FRANCISCO, WRITING THE FOREWORD to my report. I couldn't finish it before the trip, but this was never going to be a holiday anyway. I'm here for work. This is just another routine delay.

This isn't my first time here, so I don't need to get out and see the town. Not that I did any sightseeing the first time around. I planted myself in a coffee shop and tapped away on my laptop—same as I'm doing now.

It's the same everywhere I go. Ever since I quit my job to focus on my current endeavour, I've had to get out of the house to get anything done. Even if I set up an office at home, it wouldn't change anything. I'd end up sleeping all day, or maybe sitting in the kitchen and drinking. Neither is a good way to make a living, so I'd still have to force myself to get up and go out.

Fortunately, I'm too timid to make a fool of myself in public, so I always manage to keep things on an even keel.

Wherever I land, my next stop is the coffee shop. Once I've found my spot, that's where I go. I don't question it. Sometimes I'll go to a city I haven't visited in a few years only to find my usual place gone. I'll stand there frozen for a moment or two, at a loss.

I don't really like to travel. But it's not the journey I have a problem with. It's the passing through. I've never had any interest in seeing the sights. Watching the people, on the other hand, can be a pleasure. I like to keep an eye on how the crowd shifts from day to day, hour by hour. No single moment can give you the full picture.

When I have the time, I walk around, internalizing the lie of the land as if learning my way around the shelves of a bookshop.

I try to work on my report, but nothing comes to mind. Just a completely unrelated string of ideas.

I should be over my jet lag by now, but my head's like a sieve. It shouldn't make any difference where I am, but with distance my body stiffens up and my mind goes slack. It takes a while to adjust. The letters swim before my eyes, they clump together. As I look over what I'd written before the flight, it's hard to believe that I was the one who put these words down. There's this strange tension inside me, making me think slower than usual. I can prove it, too: at the coffee shop, I always work in two-hour sessions, and it's taking me twice as many sessions to finish the same amount of work.

That's how bad it is when I'm reading over what I've written. When it's time to actually do the work, everything falls apart. The text crumbles and I can't remember the previous line. I can patch the tear, but I can't predict how that intervention will affect the whole. I can see it coming apart at the seams, rips in the fabric leading to even more rips. But these holes were completely invisible to me pre-flight—these tears opening up in the present progressive.

Disturbingly, there's no way to tell what it is that's coming apart: the lines I'd written at some point in the past or my mind in the present.

Tampering with the past is bound to set off a chain reaction. If I felt that this destruction might lead to some new order, I'd be tempted to revamp the entire thing, but given that, at present, I can only see it moving inexorably in the direction of collapse, even swapping out a single word seems like a bridge too far. When you know that any action you take will result in unbridled chaos, the best thing to do is to do nothing at all. If there's no hope for improvement, why bother getting involved? Isn't that why people leave ancient ruins the way they are?

When I was a child, I took a shine to solid objects.

I wanted to be a gem-cutter when I grew up. It wasn't the sparkle that drew me in; it was the feeling of dissatisfaction. I can remember cutting out photos of solitaire rings from ads tucked inside the newspaper and laying them on the carpet. The brilliance of the gem on the flyer, and the flustered gem cut loose from its surroundings. Where's that difference come from? To be honest, I still don't get it.

When I was small, I'd play with pictures of shiny objects and bring home every reflective or light-catching piece of junk I found. That's why they used to call me *magpie*.

My thoughts keep drifting.

To continue where the wind carries me—I've always thought the brilliant cut was a strange choice. The bottom's pointy for no good reason. That's what I thought even when I was a child. Why put a stone into a setting like that just to carry it around? The cut does nothing for the gem. Why can't a ring be a ring and a gem be a gem? I still think that if we could get away from trying to adorn the human form, we could find more beautiful ways of cutting stones.

I used to think that gems, knitting, embroidery, words, and equations were essentially the same thing, but now I'm not so sure. It still feels like they share the same root, but there's something different about the root itself. Back then, I thought what they had in common was their hardness, but now I'm inclined to think it's their softness. I can't explain it, but I've started to suspect that there's no such thing as hardness, that there's nothing but motion, and hardness is only something we perceive when multiple objects happen to align. Like when you're watching the spokes of a bicycle wheel and, for an instant, it looks like the wheel isn't turning at all.

I made this trip to hand in my report to the A. A. Abrams Institute; we're supposed to show up in person once a year. My assignment: searching for Tomoyuki Tomoyuki. The project hasn't stopped—even after Abrams's death. Incorporating sometimes produces this peculiar form of immortality.

Abrams hired quite a few agents to look for Tomoyuki Tomoyuki. When you're hunting for a person who's always at least one step ahead, someone who makes a habit of moving on without leaving their next address, your best bet is strength in numbers. Because, by the time an agent catches wind of our target, he's long gone; the names he leaves on his contracts are all bogus. Wandering from place to place, he opts for row houses where he barely meets his neighbours, or places where the comings and goings of people are frequent and unpredictable. He never lives with roommates, nor does he rent the sort of apartment that would require a guarantor. Sometimes he'll make himself at home in an abandoned building, leaving his pursuers with no way to connect the dots. He uses a variety of aliases with banks as the information they ask for is easy to falsify. The only reason people typically don't bother is because there's nothing to be gained. Because there's no good reason to fool around with the system, we assume it's foolproof—but move house and you'll be stunned by the elephant-sized loopholes in the process. Seeing as we have no evidence to claim that Tomoyuki Tomoyuki is any kind of criminal, we have no right to request his ATM records from the bank.

Even now, once every three years or so, agents find another site that had been occupied by Tomoyuki Tomoyuki, but not in the order in which he moved. They stumble upon some lost chapter from his past—a discovery through which his travels are rewritten yet again.

How Tomoyuki Tomoyuki makes his living remains a mystery. The most convincing theory is that he's sitting on a substantial family fortune. Otherwise, how could he afford to be on the move all the time? Even if he could take advantage of a favourable exchange rate to move from one place to the next, the cycle would grind to a halt at some point if he had to keep making money during his travels.

Some have theorized that Tomoyuki Tomoyuki is working as an interpreter. Others believe he's a translator. There are still numerous minor languages in the world that need to pass through a series of other languages when being translated. There's something to be said for the argument that it's more economical to hire one exceptional polyglot rather than a cadre of serviceable linguists. Or perhaps Tomoyuki Tomoyuki is travelling the world in the employ of a wealthy jet-setter—someone much like Abrams. Whatever the case, all parties agree, there seems to be no rhyme or reason to Tomoyuki Tomoyuki's movements.

So: how exactly are we supposed to search for someone so erratic? To put it bluntly, no one knows. And that's why every agent at the institute—our exact numbers are unknown even to me—is given a net.

That's what I do: wave my little net around and report what I catch. When we catch something that has material form, we mail it in. When we catch an idea, we write it up in a report and send that in. Some agents use their nets to catch actual insects and submit specimen cases, but when my handler showed me one of these cases, I took one look at the meticulous labelling and decided that wasn't the path for me.

Why give us nets?

For the most part, the institute has kept us in the dark. We're given only the most basic instructions: use your net, send us what you catch. The exact nature of how we carry out our duties is left to us—any request for clarification is met with a closed door.

At this point, we can only imagine what might or might not have hatched in Abrams's head, but my best guess goes something like this: when we travel, our ideas escape and float free. Capture one of these ideas and you should be able to identify its erstwhile owner.

Ordinary people produce commensurately ordinary thoughts, but someone like Tomoyuki Tomoyuki must shed ideas of a wholly unique quality.

At a minimum, should you find such an idea in the wild, there would be a strong likelihood that Tomoyuki Tomoyuki had been in the area at some point in the not-too-distant past.

I don't know why the rich do the things they do—it's foolish to speculate about what's going on in the minds of others to begin with—but I sincerely doubt I'm far off. In the long run, we're slowly eating our way through Abrams's fortune, but that doesn't seem to be a major concern for anyone involved. Call it a slow-motion redistribution of wealth.

I couldn't tell you what it takes to become an agent with the institute.

Much like MI6, job openings are posted for all the world to see. Fill out the form, pop it in the postbox, and they send you a butterfly net. When I applied, I got a thousand US dollars along with the brusque message: SUBMIT WHAT YOU CATCH. I received no other instructions, so I figured this had to be some sort of pro bationary period. I once mentioned what I was doing to a friend, who then sent in an application, thinking it sounded like an easy way to earn some cash. Before long, they got a postcard with a terse rejection on the back—which means that the institute has a screening process of some kind.

I send them what I catch. My expenses and whatever fee they decide to give me are then deposited directly into my bank account. In terms of interaction, there's pretty much none to speak of. After my first few submissions, I signed a contract, but the documents were so detailed that I still haven't actually read them.

I don't know how they evaluate the reports we submit, but in my case, I can make ends meet as long as I complete two or three submissions a month. On rare occasions, they'll turn down what I turn in. Other times, I'll receive a larger payment than expected. In the end, it all evens out. I've heard a few stories about agents being fired without warning, for no apparent reason, but the institute offers a severance package generous enough that no one ever complains.

When you're in a slump, they recommend taking a trip.

If the institute had its way, all of us would travel non-stop. But, having lost their own founder to deep-vein thrombosis, the organization isn't in a position to insist. Speed frees ideas from the body—it's an odd notion, to be sure, and those of us in the field aren't required to subscribe to it. All that matters is that we get results, and that doesn't seem to have anything to do with belief. Really, you could spend your days just strolling around your neighbourhood, swinging your net, and do fine. It doesn't look like they're keeping a close eye on us, so I don't think it would even make a difference if I went around without my net, but I still feel like I'm being tested somehow, so I end up bring-ing it along anyway.

At first, I thought they had to be joking, but I called their bluff, emptied out my savings, and took a trip to Argentina. When I saw they'd covered my expenses without batting an eye, it finally dawned on me: the institute means business. They genuinely want to find Tomoyuki Tomoyuki, and they have the utmost confidence in their methods. Or, at a minimum, inertia is keeping the enterprise in orbit.

I've entertained the idea that the institute is using its agents to simulate Tomoyuki Tomoyuki's existence.

Even now, I have to wonder whether 'Under a Cat' is a true Tomoyuki Tomoyuki. To be honest, part of the reason I decided to translate the piece was to see if I could pick up on any traces of imposture. The more I find out about the author, the more unlikely it seems that he would have opted for a language like *Latino sine flexione*.

If an agent with no linguistic talent were trying to pass off some work as Tomoyuki Tomoyuki's, it would make the most sense to go with a language that has no speakers. As long as you maintained a modicum of grammaticality, no one would have a clue. Ultimately, however, I was unable to detect any signs of subterfuge.

The idea that the institute might want its agents to take up the task of producing Tomoyuki Tomoyuki's body of work is a tempting one. At one point, I tried writing an original piece, *To Be Read Only on an Airplane*, also in *Latino sine flexione*, then submitted it to the institute to see how they'd respond. I figured maybe they wanted us to add to the total number of *Latino sine flexione* works in the collection. And, on some level, I thought it might be fun if that kind of submission caught on among the agents.

I was paid for the piece—but far less than I'd hoped. Given that my subsequent submissions, a report titled 'Notes on Impersonating Tomoyuki Tomoyuki' and my translation of 'Under a Cat', were rewarded handsomely by comparison, I have to believe that the institute had not in fact been looking for someone to author new works under Tomoyuki Tomoyuki's name. I later realized that if I was going to present a piece of writing as an undiscovered manuscript, it would have to match Tomoyuki Tomoyuki's hand, but there was actually no need for what I turned in to be original material. A translation from an obscure language would work just fine.

The institute overpaying for useless submissions all the while underpaying for what they're really after would be an effective strategy for concealing their true intentions. Even better if they were to mix things up from time to time. I still haven't ruled out the possibility that they're simply determining our payments with a roll of the dice.

If you took the net-swinging out of the equation and reduced what we do to its simplest possible terms, we're selling the ideas that pop into our heads—not too bizarre a business, if you think about it. There are plenty of people out there doing the same thing. Every so often, I'll send in designs for a device I've dreamt up: a perpetual-motion machine I'd glimpsed in a daydream, etc. Collect enough material and one or two ideas are bound to pay off. After all, isn't that how Abrams's own fortune was built? Going around collecting ideas for idiosyncratic inventions?

Is the institute out to realize the late Abrams's dying wish of finding Tomoyuki Tomoyuki, or is it aiming to turn out an ever-growing army of mass-produced Abramses? Part of me wonders whether anybody at the institute knows. It's possible that anyone who knew the truth is gone now—or maybe there was no such soul there to begin with. As anticlimactic as that would be, perhaps rules and regulations alone have been keeping the operation in motion.

As I sit in this coffee shop writing, the people around me are stringing all kinds of words together, freely and easily. What they say is partially comprehensible to me, but at the same time it strikes me as nothing but sound. I've tried following in Tomoyuki Tomoyuki's footsteps, using his method for picking up languages, but apparently writing down the sounds that enter my ears isn't my forte. Asked to choose one sound over another, I wouldn't know where to begin. Sometimes I wonder if this lack of strong feelings is why I've never been any good at languages.

I always write my reports in Japanese. The institute doesn't seem to mind which language we use in our submissions, but Japanese is the only language that I can fully utilize in its written form. They probably recognize that requiring agents to write in an unfamiliar language wouldn't help their bottom line. It makes more sense to hire specialists to translate the work we produce.

Whenever I'm abroad, in a place where I'm confronted by the powerlessness of my native tongue, my linguistic landscape grows wild. Outside sounds break in like a sandstorm, blasting away any loose leaves and branches. In response, vines and tendrils shoot up in futile flourishes until all that's left is some sort of no man's land—a place where I have no idea whether I'm moving forward or backward.

In a language without users, you're free to write whatever you want, however you want. But, as soon as you think that what you've written might fall into someone else's hands, the words start to stir. You begin to wonder whether you should explain how to read the writing itself, and your attention moves farther and farther away from the content. You start to feel the need to explain what's written there. There's a difference between making something clear and indicating what is being made clear. You find yourself plagued by the fear that maybe that difference isn't the same from one language to another.

Imagine a story—one that's utterly meaningless, contradictory, incoherent. What if there's a language somewhere in the world that would render that story logically sound? A language in which that story would become perfectly ordinary, all its strangeness concealed from view?

There's no need to imagine anything extreme: just take a look at our everyday conversations. We tune each other out, blithely contradict ourselves, interject and interrupt, repeat and repeat ourselves. In the moment, this registers as dialogue, but if those sounds were to be transcribed directly, the results would be unintelligible.

A language with backdoors built into the grammar.

"A daughter gives birth to her mother."

A sentence like this one contains a semantic contradiction, but the issue can be resolved by tinkering with the lines around it. Throw in an extra word or two, maybe "time machine", and you're covered. Or perhaps the contradiction splits in two and vanishes.

"The next sentence is lying. The previous sentence is telling the truth."

Skim these lines and there's no cause for alarm. But take a harder look at the pair and a different picture emerges. If the second sentence really is lying, as the first one claims, that means the first one has to be telling a lie, and if the first sentence is lying, then the second one had to be telling the truth all along.

And yet, there's no rule stating that such contradictions have to be generated or resolved at the word level. What if there were a language in which these operations took place in the grammar itself?

Would it be so strange to have a language in which the grammar transforms every time an inconsistency arises between different tellings of the same story?

What if we simply haven't noticed those shifts?

And if that movement were to end up caught in a loop, unable to break free, wouldn't that spell the end of the tale?

* * *

At the front desk of the A. A. Abrams Institute, I collect my annual evaluation and turn in the report I'd been working on right up to the last minute. It's so similar to all my other reports that I feel a little guilty, but I should probably feel this way every time I send something in. The old woman behind the counter takes the envelope, tears it open and flips through my report. I bet she can't read a lick of Japanese.

"Looks good," she says, smiling as she taps the report against the counter to straighten the pages.

I flip over this year's evaluation and run my eyes over the chart on the back: details of monthly payments and mysterious markings for each report I've submitted—in Latin, in Japanese, in Burmese, in Ktav Ashuri. Even if I asked, the woman wouldn't be able to shed any light on what these symbols mean, so I don't bother. I've never known how they evaluate my writing in the first place, so it only makes sense for the feedback itself to be inscrutable as well.

The clerk pulls out a thick folder, opening it so that I can't see the contents. She looks at my file, then at me. This is the only conceivable reason for our annual face-to-face visits. They're checking to make sure that we truly exist, that we are in fact the same people we were last time around. It's strange. There are some things that no amount of data can prove, but only take a split second to confirm in person.

The woman nudges a black ink pad towards me. I'm pretty sure this violates a law or two, but I don't care enough to make a fuss. I press each finger where the woman indicates.

She asks:

"Think we'll find him?"

I answer back:

"Think we'll find him?"

This is how we communicate. We shrug our shoulders in unison, exchanging half-smiles.

"The director said your last submission was fascinating. It was a story about using a butterfly net to collect ideas for stories?"

"I didn't come up with that one."

It was a translation. Didn't get much money for it, either.

"I wrote the one in the envelope. But I take it you won't be reading it."

"Nope."

I pull the little net out of my breast pocket and wave it in front of the woman's eyes.

She knits her brow, then forces a smile. After some

time, she claps her hands together and brings our staring contest to an end.

"Well, see you again next year," she says as she gives my file one final glance. "Mister... Tomoyuki Tomoyuki?" she adds, lifting her eyebrows as she pretends to trip over that familiar sequence of simple syllables.

I start to brush away her little joke with my right hand, then, thinking better of it, catch it in my net.

V

I COLLECT THE REPORT FROM THE MAN, THEN WATCH HIM WALK
away. He waves at me before disappearing through
the door. I stand behind the counter for some time,
then head slowly up the stairs. The doors lining the
hallway are labelled in a variety of ways. Abrams cast
a wide net, building a collection that expanded in so
many different directions. The records documenting
my activities take up only a fraction of the total space.
My rooms start at the far end of the hall, and they seem
to be taking up more of the floor as time goes on, slowly
but surely eating up additional square footage. I choose
a door, open it, and flick on the light.

The clutter of craft supplies on the table is over-
whelming; it takes me a while to get my bearings.

I'm ensnared by a net that takes the shape of a
spider's web.

I squint at the lacemaking bobbins fanned out
around it. To the uninitiated, this contraption probably

looks like a mechanical calculator from some ancient civilization. It's the epitome of simplicity—and yet unbelievably intricate. How long has it been since I put this down? I run my fingers over the knots, then pick up the bobbins and roll them around in my palm, waiting for the lace to speak to me—waiting for the atmosphere to resequence its sweetness. The Egyptian desert sweeps in, bringing with it the scent of fresh mint.

Thus begins my counterfeit journey.

It's no coincidence that I found myself at the institute eventually. This place was made for me. Made to do what I never could—to collect me, to bring all of my pieces together.

A jumbled mishmash of forgotten pasts, waiting impatiently to be interpreted.

"I can read textiles," I said. "I know they're not texts, but I can read them... As long as it's the right piece."

That comment piqued the interest of my interviewer.

A team at the institute had been trying to classify the motley objects they'd received from agents in the field, but hadn't managed to get beyond the initial cataloguing. They were in over their heads. As the institute's main focus has always been my writing, the other materials they've hauled in have generally gotten short shrift. Is this technique typical of coastal or inland work? How does the twist or the tension applied to the thread differ between this country and that one?

"I can tell the difference," I said.

They gave me a few tests, which I passed, and now I work at the institute as a special officer. The pay's paltry, to say the least, but I only need to come in for about one month out of six. They also give me a modest allowance—for "research expenses"—which makes it that much easier to sustain my constant travels.

Initially, I assumed I'd be able to get an easy read on all the pieces and tools collected here, but I was wrong. A significant portion of these items were never mine to begin with. Could it be that I've simply forgotten them? I can't rule that out, but I've stumbled over more than a few pieces that were made using methods I have no memory of.

The agents bring in various materials from the sites where they find my work, and anything that looks even vaguely related to craft ends up tossed into this space. As a result, the border between the handmade and the mass-produced blurs, and the boundary between implement and artefact wobbles. I'm sure in some cases they just buy up every object they can find in the vicinity of my rooms. Further complicating matters, the agents seem to have brazenly added more than a few creations of their own to the mix.

Between projects, I dive into something I've written—or something written by somebody else. I don't know that many languages, but I recognize my own writing no matter what the language is. The same goes for all the things I've created. I can read my own handiwork, if in the most formless of ways. When I'm reading, and only when I'm reading, the language comes back to me; that place appears in my mind, my knowledge of that craft is revived.

A book that can be read only when travelling.

A journey that can be taken only when reading.

A craft rediscovered in a book that can only be read during a journey that can only be taken while reading a book.

The written work teased from the resulting textile.

I work the net, manipulating the bobbins without even needing to think. How much more lace can I make before night returns?

There's actually someone I'm hoping to see. Part of me is clinging to the idea that, just like the lace can bring back lost memories, it might be able to bring back a person I used to know. But that's a tall order.

After all, the people I've met aren't *me*. What are the odds that I'll find someone who isn't me inside my own imagination?

Still, I ask—what about the one who knitted two-person patterns with me? We were almost like instruments to each other, weren't we? If we were in fact devices and not people, then we would have ended up here eventually, either of our own volition or through the work of the agents. Then again, I don't even remember who that person is anymore. If I saw them somewhere, I probably wouldn't recognize them. Even if we met face to face, I doubt I'd know.

A name repeated is an invitation.

Trying to pick up where I left off, I unwittingly set something new in motion, and what's mine is infiltrated by something that isn't mine at all.

I spend my nights writing.

I used to read only my own writing, but since coming to the institute, I've started reading others' work as well. Right now, I'm looking at the manuscript submitted by the man who came in today—the one who's not Tomoyuki Tomoyuki. I couldn't tell you what it says. I don't know the language, and when I want to understand something written by a stranger in a strange language, I have to go to the place where it's spoken.

But the words on the page still have an effect. The same goes for the quality of the paper itself, the pulp fibres, the marks on the envelope. I document my vague impressions as they come to me.

I take my fountain pen in my hand.

The tip catches on something—something a little hard. It's like it's tripped over a silver wire, the nib taking off in an unexpected direction.

Gemstones.

First the word, then a question mark.

Or maybe glass.

For a moment, I wonder if it's about glassmaking, then decide otherwise.

A piece of lace doesn't have the same feel as a piece of writing about lace, the textile being nothing more than a product of the text. Just as the texture of lace differs from that of the hands that made it.

As if unearthing a dinosaur bone with a fossil brush, I trace the outline of the report. Gemstones? Glass? An equation? One possibility, then another. With each stroke of the brush, my certainty wavers. Each discovery erases the last. There's a preciseness to the object that makes it feel artificial—then again, what if it's a mineral formation that simply gives the impression of being man-made?

I have no way of finding out what language this manuscript is written in. As I copy it out, it almost seems like it isn't a human language at all. Not one with any living users anyway.

My hand falls still, but the pen keeps going. Then I realize:

These lines make up some powerful kind of curse.

A curse designed to take the air out of my words—to tie up my thinking and freeze the blood in my veins. All the disguises I've ever assumed break out of me and turn to crystal, shooting up like trees. Before my eyes, their branches transform into a labyrinth of wires, surrounding me. Countless crystalline butterflies fill the air like falling leaves. They crash into each other and shatter into bits. New butterflies keep coming, colliding almost as soon as they appear.

A gust of wind blows glass dust into my face. I shake my head, brush off my clothes, and look around. I'm standing alone, in an endless, lifeless realm bereft of language. No more figures of speech—I'm completely on my own.

There's a door in the distance. Around it, I see no flat surface that might be a wall. Just the door, standing among the trees. Beyond the frame and off to one side is an old man, stamping his feet like an actor waiting for his turn to appear on stage.

The man pushes at the door with the tip of his cane, then steps through with a large butterfly net over his shoulder, moving from left to right. He turns back to look at the portal, then circles around the freestanding frame. After going through the door a few more times, the man takes a couple of steps back and glares at it. Shrugging exaggeratedly, he gives the jamb a disapproving whack.

Then, shaking his head in exasperation, he holds up his index finger as if to say, *Be right there.*

The old man swings his cane at the butterflies fluttering through the air, beating them back as he leaps around the trees. It doesn't seem like he's coming my way—then there he is. He seems surprised to find himself there as he removes his hat. At first, I think the gesture has to be a salutation—a greeting meant for me—but he immediately proceeds to unbutton the collar of his shirt to let some air in. The man's frowning as if he's just swallowed a nasty memory. He rolls a couple of words around on his tongue, testing them, then swallows and clears his throat. Once his voice is warmed up, he launches right in:

"You went a little too far, didn't you? Drew too much attention to yourself. If people notice you, they start making up stories. Next thing you know, here we are."

"Can we talk here, even if there's no language?" I ask haltingly.

Lifting his eyebrows in amusement, the old man asks back: "Does it pose some sort of problem if what we're doing isn't talking?"

"Maybe not," I say, acquiescing.

The air here is so cold, so thin, that I can't find the words to draw out a longer string of words. The old man nods as if I were a student of his. He takes a deep breath and fills his lungs, then speaks:

"I know this one: Latin. I had to memorize it when I was young. The inflections are all wrong, but this is no mistake. After all, they're consistently wrong. Someone's done this on purpose. Maybe they tried to squeeze it into the shape of a language they'd grown up with, or had certain expressions they were desperate to preserve... Or perhaps they did it out of metric necessity..."

The old man closes his eyes and listens to the echo of his own words as they pass through the trees.

"No, I see it now. They wanted to make the language

as simple as possible, so they pruned it down to its bare branches. That was their intention, but the intervention has only made the language that much harder to speak."

As the old man's voice vibrates through the air, butterflies shatter, bursting into echoes of his words, then disappearing among the trees.

"No one else could come to a place like this," the man says proudly. "Nobody but me." Then, after looking around the forest of overgrown columns, he turns back to me.

"But never mind that. As I was saying, you've gone too far. Wasting your time making all this worthless junk."

The old man reaches out to strike another butterfly that has ventured too close.

"These things may be pretty to look at sitting on a desk, but they're far too unwieldy to be flying around like this. They'll contradict each other until there's nothing left." The old man lets out a short grunt and sits down. "But if that's what you want, I won't get in your way..."

I shake my head.

He glances up at me with a sympathetic look, then turns away.

"Well, let's just table that for the time being. That's not why we're here. I hear you've got a knack for nets—nets of all kinds."

"What kind of net are you looking for?" I ask immediately, by force of habit.

"One designed to capture a particular type of butterfly. There are nets out there that can do the job, but they catch much more than they should. It's led to trouble here, there and everywhere. Who can even say where to begin to set things straight? But maybe it doesn't matter where you begin, just as long as you do..."

Unsure what the old man is getting at, I give him a quizzical look. There are all kinds of butterflies in the world. If I'm supposed to make something for a specific purpose, I'll need details. Or, in the absence of specifics, a feeling, or an emotion...

"In other words," the old man continues, "I need a net to catch butterflies and butterflies alone. One that will catch any butterfly—real or imaginary."

I think for a little while, then point at one of the butterflies gliding through the air. I begin to say, "Are these..." I want to confirm whether or not the net should be able to catch them, too. Even if they are artificial, I figure, they might still count.

"Those aren't butterflies," the old man snorts. "Let those gimcrack imitations do as they please. Catching them only leads to more trouble. Do you follow?"

"...I do."

"All right then."

As he watches me move my head up and down and side to side at the same time, the old man nods in satisfaction, then starts to reminisce.

"It's only a hobby now, but I once studied butterflies for a living... Then, mere moments ago, someone brought me the strangest specimen. Or at least that's the way it was presented to me. Regrettable, but what's been written is writ. Still, I'd be lying if I said it didn't make my blood boil. I told the man I had to use the restroom and slipped out. What he'd brought me was a rare butterfly that can only be caught using a very special kind of net. Still following?"

"I think so."

"Somehow I doubt it," he says, snorting again. "Do you know what a scholar feels when presented with a find of this kind—something truly remarkable?"

"Admiration...?"

"Not even close!" the old man exclaims, flinging his arms around and waving his cane in the air. "Indignation! He's furious that the discovery wasn't his to make. How much better it is for a specimen of this quality to remain undiscovered than to be found by someone else!"

"Greed," I say, a frown spreading across my face.

The old man lets out a hearty laugh.

"Naturally! It's only natural! But I have no interest in claiming someone else's work as my own. I just want to level the playing field. And that's where this net comes in. Mind you, I don't need it to be especially strong, so long as it can catch the butterfly in question. Rest assured, what I'm proposing isn't a bad deal for you, either.

"After all, you were the one who made the net that catches every last thing to sail through the air. And that's why things took the turn they did, and then kept on turning until we ended up here, starting over again, but from the other end of the beginning."

"Now I think you've lost me."

"I don't doubt it. This hasn't been made to be understood. A handful of pieces tossed onto a chessboard does not a chess problem make. A sheet of gridded paper with random squares blacked out isn't always a crossword puzzle. Frankly, I don't understand it myself. And if I can't comprehend it, then I have to wonder whether there's anybody on this planet who can."

"I'll see what I can do."

Deciding there's nothing more I can learn from the man, I give a light shrug. In the end, someone has to do the work.

"Time to tie up loose ends," the old man says as he lies down on his back.

Now on my own, I scan my surroundings. Among the trees, where it seems like there ought to be some grass, I find fine wire, growing in tangles like native silver. When I touch it, the wire bends with ease, but doesn't spring back. I take a pair of scissors out of my pocket and snip off a strand. I put it between my front teeth and bite down, leaving a mark. The material has a metallic scent, but calls nothing to mind—no place, no memory.

And there you have it—with a book under his arm, the lepidopterist returns to the table.

Shooting a sly smile at the man gazing rapturously at the butterfly, the lepidopterist hides the book behind his back, straightens his smile, then comes around to face him.

"So she's a new species of imaginary butterfly?" the man asks back—because that's the scene to which the lepidopterist returned when he slipped through the door. After making a little pit stop on the way back, of course.

What was this man's name again? Oh, right—Abrams. By this point, he's shown up so many times he's pretty much a regular. Then again, he seems just a little less *regular* with every iteration. Much like this rickety stage. Too easy, the old man smiles to himself. Who says what's done can't be undone? All these backdoors left wide open: set phrases, relative pronouns, meter... I didn't think I'd be the one to wrap this up, but all the other players have already exited the arena.

"Yes indeed," the old man says impassively.

"My very own discovery," Abrams replies, elated by the thought.

"Well, I wouldn't go that far," the old man says as he pulls out the book and opens it in front of Abrams.

Beneath the inscription, "To Véra", is the sketch of a butterfly labelled "Arlequinus arlequinus ♂".

The butterfly on the rim of Abrams's glass flaps its wings and lands right next to the image on the page. As if the butterfly and the sketch were on opposite sides of a mirror.

"You've discovered the first known *female*, but the species itself is already known. I happen to have caught the male myself, just the other day. Still, in the grand scheme of things, it's early enough to call it a new species..."

"But, but..." Abrams says before angrily swallowing his words. "That's a different story..."

"Is that right? And what story was it you heard, and where? Besides…"

Just then, as the lepidopterist reaches out for the butterfly on the page, Abrams's face changes colour: first red, then blue. Without hesitation, the old man tightens his fingers around the butterfly's body. Abrams jolts up, but in that same moment the harlequin slips through the lepidopterist's grasp and flies away, as if the old man hadn't touched it at all.

"You didn't catch this butterfly," the old man declares, his fingers shimmering with butterfly dust as he rubs them together. "You're merely tagging along."

Abrams scrambles to grab his hat and swings it down over his target. For a moment or two, the butterfly vanishes from view, then re-emerges as it floats through the hat. All the while flashing its kaleidoscopic pattern without a care in the world.

As Abrams lets out a frustrated groan and falls back in his chair, the old man leaps up and produces a small silver net. Leaving his cane behind, he moves with startling speed, capturing the airborne butterfly with a quick flick of his wrist. Carefully holding the net shut between two fingers, the old man walks back over—now slowly. In the hold of the net, the butterfly flaps its wings.

"Fear not—all isn't lost. You can have one of these, but which will it be? The harlequin butterfly or the harlequin-catching net?"

Holding the butterfly in one hand and the net in the other, the old man waits for Abrams's answer.

"I want…" Abrams begins, sinking into his chair before finally whispering, "I want the net that catches ideas."

"So be it. Mind how you use it, lest it be the end of you."

The old man presses the net into Abrams's open hand, releases the butterfly and sends me off with a wave.

Now free, I return to my journey—the search for my next host.

I make my way skyward, undoing past and future with each beat of my wings—those things that are supposed to have happened already, those things that are yet to happen.

I turn front into back and back into front, the diamonds on my wings changing colour with every motion I make.

As I gather altitude, the distance folding beneath my wings, I'm drawn to a steel bird in flight.

A passenger is flipping through the pages of a paperback with a frown on his face. He drops the book into his lap and closes his eyes. I know this man. As I try to remember where I've seen him before, I slip into his head, clearing space and pushing out whatever language is stuffed inside. It's not in my nature to remember, to think. This body of mine isn't equipped to do that. To access these functions, I need to borrow a head.

Inside the man's head, I deposit a single egg.

Once my child leaves her egg, she'll feed on words.

This is how I create.

After all my peregrinations, against all odds, I found a mate. I must have—it's the only way I could have produced an egg. This is why our species is so rare. We've maintained our numbers somehow, but our reproductive process is in constant flux, the specifics a mystery even to us. In each instance, we need to work out the details for ourselves, to dream up a method to fit the circumstances.

After all, there's a right time, place and strategy for everything, and anything that claims to work everywhere can only be subpar—some kind of sham.

Each new setting necessitates a new method of reproduction.

What about a book that can be read only when travelling?

Slowly, the idea starts to take shape inside the man's mind. For now, I have to keep moving, but I'll find out what took place here soon enough—when our child takes flight.

Among the infinite number of other butterflies, I'll know her right away by the pattern of her wings.

MORE FROM PUSHKIN'S
JAPANESE NOVELLA SERIES

KAORI FUJINO

NAILS AND EYES

KAZUSHIGE ABE

NIPPONIA NIPPON

NATSUKO IMAMURA
AUTHOR OF THE WOMAN IN THE PURPLE SKIRT

**THIS IS AMIKO,
DO YOU COPY?**

NISHIOKA KYŌDAI

KAFKA

TOH ENJOE

**HARLEQUIN
BUTTERFLY**

KUMI KIMURA

**SOMEONE
TO WATCH
OVER YOU**

JAPANESE FICTION
AVAILABLE AND COMING SOON
FROM PUSHKIN PRESS

MS ICE SANDWICH
Mieko Kawakami

MURDER IN THE AGE OF ENLIGHTENMENT
Ryūnosuke Akutagawa

THE HONJIN MURDERS
Seishi Yokomizo

RECORD OF A NIGHT TOO BRIEF
Hiromi Kawakami

SPRING GARDEN
Tomoka Shibasaki

COIN LOCKER BABIES
Ryu Murakami

THE DECAGON HOUSE MURDERS
Yukito Ayatsuji

SLOW BOAT
Hideo Furukawa

THE HUNTING GUN
Yasushi Inoue

SALAD ANNIVERSARY
Machi Tawara

THE CAKE TREE IN THE RUINS
Akiyuki Nosaka